12/96

YOUNG CAM JANSEN
and the
Missing Cookie

A Viking Easy-to-Read

by David A. Adler
illustrated by Susanna Natti

VIKING

VIKING
Published by the Penguin Group
Penguin Books USA Inc., 375 Hudson Street, New York, New York 10014, U.S.A.
Penguin Books Ltd, 27 Wrights Lane, London W8 5TZ, England
Penguin Books Australia Ltd, Ringwood, Victoria, Australia
Penguin Books Canada Ltd, 10 Alcorn Avenue, Toronto, Ontario, Canada M4V 3B2
Penguin Books (N.Z.) Ltd, 182-190 Wairau Road, Auckland 10, New Zealand

Penguin Books Ltd, Registered Offices: Harmondsworth, Middlesex, England

First published in 1996 by Viking, a division of Penguin Books USA Inc.

1   3   5   7   9   10   8   6   4   2

Text copyright © David A. Adler, 1996
Illustrations copyright © Susanna Natti, 1996
All rights reserved

LIBRARY OF CONGRESS CATALOGING-IN-PUBLICATION DATA

Adler, David A.
Young Cam Jansen and the missing cookie / by David A. Adler ;
pictures by Susanna Natti.   p.   cm.—(A Viking easy-to-read)
Summary: Eight-year-old sleuth Cam Jansen uses her photographic memory
to discover what happened to a classmate's missing cookie.
ISBN 0-670-86772-1 (hc)
[1. Mystery and detective stories 2. Cookies—Fiction.]
I. Natti, Susanna, ill. II. Title. III. Series.
PZ7.A2615Yr 1996 [Fic]—dc20 95-46462 CIP AC

Printed in Singapore
Set in Bookman

Reading Level 1.7

CONTENTS

1. Click! 6
2. The Missing Cookie 14
3. Stop Him! 17
4. The Thief 24

1. CLICK!

Rrrr!

The school bell rang.

It was time for lunch.

Mrs. Dee told the class,

"Don't go yet.

First copy your homework."

Mrs. Dee wrote six math problems

on the chalkboard.

The children in the class copied them.

But not Cam Jansen.

Cam looked at the board.

She closed her eyes and said, "Click!"

Cam always closes her eyes

and says "Click!" when she wants

to remember something.

Then Cam opened her eyes.

She waited for her friend Eric Shelton.

He was copying the homework.

When he was done,

Cam and Eric went to the lunchroom.

Jason Jones sat with Cam and Eric.

Jason said to Cam,

"You didn't copy the homework."

Cam smiled.

"I don't need to copy it," Cam said.

"I remember it."

Jason said, "No one can remember
all those numbers."

Eric said, "Oh, yes.

Cam has an amazing memory."

Cam closed her eyes and said, "Click!"

Then she read off all the numbers.

"So what!" Jason said.

"I didn't bring my notebook.

Maybe those are the wrong numbers."

Cam's eyes were still closed.

She said, "Click" again.

"Jason," she said,

"you're wearing a polka-dot shirt.

There are seven polka dots

on your shirt pocket."

Jason counted the dots on his pocket.

Cam was right.

"And there are lots of short white hairs on your right sleeve."

"Those are Emily's hairs," Jason said.

"She's my dog.

I played with her this morning."

Jason brushed off some of the hairs.

Then he said,

"You didn't remember all that.

You were peeking.

I'll prove it."

Cam's eyes were still closed.

Jason took a piece of paper

from his pocket.

He wrote, "Say yes

if you want a chocolate chip cookie."

Jason held the paper in front of Cam.

She didn't say yes.

But Eric said yes.

"No," Jason told him.

"I wrote this only for Cam.

And if she didn't say yes

to a chocolate chip cookie,

maybe she's not peeking.

Maybe she really does have

an amazing memory."

2. THE MISSING COOKIE

Cam opened her eyes.

"My memory is like a camera," Cam said.

"I have a picture in my head

of everything I've seen.

'Click!' is the sound my camera makes

when it takes a picture.

And I say 'Click!' again

when I want to remember something."

Cam's real name is Jennifer.

But because of her great memory,

people started to call her "the Camera."

Then "the Camera" became just Cam.

Cam took a cheese sandwich

out of her lunch bag.

Eric took out a jelly sandwich.

Jason had a lunch box.

He opened it and took out

an egg salad sandwich.

"Hey!" Jason said.

"Where is my chocolate chip cookie?"

Cam and Eric looked

into Jason's lunch box.

There were cookie crumbs inside it.

But no cookie.

Jason said, "Last night

I put the cookie in my lunch box.

Now it's gone.

Someone stole my chocolate chip cookie."

3. STOP HIM!

"But who would steal a cookie?" Cam asked.

Jason said, "During class

my lunch box was in the closet.

Anyone could have opened it.

Maybe Pam took the cookie.

She sits near the closet.

For lunch she only gets

a sandwich and carrot sticks."

Eric shook his head.

"It wasn't Pam," he said.

"I baked sugar cookies,

and I gave her one.

But she wouldn't eat it.

She doesn't like cookies."

Cam said, "Your sugar cookies were burned.

That's why she didn't want one."

Jason looked around the lunchroom.

"Look at Susie," he said.

Susie was eating a big round cookie.

"That may be my cookie."

Susie was at the other end of the room.

Jason walked over to her.

Cam said to Eric,

"I don't think Susie would steal."

Cam bit into her sandwich.

She sipped her milk and thought.

Jason came back to the table.

"Susie was eating an oatmeal cookie," he said.

"She baked it herself."

Cam ate some more of her sandwich.

A few crumbs dropped onto the table.

Eric told Jason, "Lots of people

have big cookies for lunch."

"Not like mine," Jason said.

"My dad made it.

It has lots and lots of chocolate chips."

Cam looked at the sandwich crumbs

that were on the table.

Then she closed her eyes

and said, "Click!"

She wanted to remember something.

Jason looked at the next table.

He saw Annie take a big cookie

from her lunch box.

Jason said, "Look at all the chocolate chips

in that cookie.

That's the cookie Dad baked for me."

Jason ran to Annie's table.

Cam opened her eyes.

"Stop him!" Cam said.

"Annie didn't take his cookie.

But I know who did."

4. THE THIEF

It was too late to stop Jason.

He was already at Annie's table.

Cam dropped her sandwich.

She ran to Annie's table.

Eric followed her.

Annie was about to eat

the chocolate chip cookie.

Cam, Eric, and Jason

were looking at Annie.

Other children were looking, too.

"My birthday is tomorrow," Annie said.

"Are you here to surprise me?

That's so nice."

"I'm not here to be nice," Jason said.

"Stop!" Cam said.

"I know who took your cookie."

"I know, too," Jason said.

"Annie took it!"

Annie looked at her cookie.

Then she said, "I took this from home.

It's mine!"

Annie bit into her chocolate chip cookie.

Cookie crumbs fell onto the table.

"Annie is right," Cam said.

"It _is_ her cookie."

Cam looked inside Annie's lunch box.

She told Eric and Jason

to look inside Annie's lunch box, too.

"It's empty," they said.

Cam said, "Now let's look

in Jason's lunch box."

Cam, Eric, and Jason

went back to their table.

They looked in Jason's lunch box.

"It's empty, too," Eric said.

"No it's not," Cam said.

She turned the lunch box upside down.

Crumbs fell onto the table.

"You had crumbs in there

because your cookie was eaten

while it was still <u>inside</u>

your lunch box."

"Who would eat a cookie that way?" Jason asked.

Cam pointed to the short white hairs

on Jason's sleeve and said,

"A dog would eat a cookie that way!"

"Of course," Jason said.

"It was Emily.

She ate my cookie.

She'll eat anything."

Cam, Eric, and Jason

finished eating their sandwiches.

Then Eric said to Jason,

"I'm sorry your cookie is gone.

You can have some of mine."

Eric gave Jason two sugar cookies.

"Thank you," said Jason.

He looked at the cookies.

He gave them back to Eric.

"You are a good friend," Jason said.

"But you are not a good baker.

Cam was right.

Your sugar cookies are burned.

Even Emily wouldn't eat them."

"Well, I would," Eric said.

And he did.